Gate of IVREL

CLAIMING RITES

Adapted and Illustrated by Jane Fancher
from the novel by C. J. Cherryh

Edited by Kay Reynolds

The Donning Company/Publishers
Norfolk/Virginia Beach • 1987

STARBLAZE GRAPHICS

Gate of Ivrel: Claiming Rites, adapted and illustrated by Jane Fancher from the novel by C. J. Cherryh, is one of the many graphic novels published by The Donning Company/Publishers. For a complete listing of our titles, please write to the address below.

The novel **Gate of Ivrel** by C. J. Cherryh is copyright by C. J. Cherryh. This graphic novel adaptation is published by arrangement with DAW Books, Inc., New York, New York.

Art and adaptation copyright© 1987 Jane Fancher.

The Donning Company/Publishers
5659 Virginia Beach Boulevard
Norfolk, Virginia 23502

First Printing July 1987

10 9 8 7 6 5 4 3 2 1

Library of Congress Cataloging-in-Publication Data

Fancher, Jane, 1952-
  Gate of Ivrel.
  Adaptation of: Gate of Ivrel/by C. J. Cherryh.
  I. Reynolds, Kay, 1951- . II. Cherryh, C. J.
Gate of Ivrel. III. Title.
PN6727.F35G3 1987   741.5'973   86-32-755
ISBN 0-89865-515-3

Printed in the United States of America

Gate of IVREL
CLAIMING RITES
INTRODUCTION

Some years ago a young artist showed me her concept sketches and her adaptation of **Gate Of Ivrel** as a graphic novel. I was immediately impressed—for one thing I *like* graphic novels, and I love looking at good artwork; but I am a much harder sell when it comes to adaptations and scripting, which get into *my* field, which is writing.

I immediately knew I was dealing with an unusual talent in Jane Fancher. One of the things I immediately thought of when Jane explained what she wanted to show me, was that **Gate Of Ivrel** is a very difficult book to do—the characters *aren't* talkative, and frequently when they do open their mouths it's only to say something completely misleading unless you know what's going on in their heads. It's a novel, in short, about a very uncommunicative partnership, in which sometimes the only way to know what's going on with them from the outside is to be in a position to see the little subtleties of expression they show only when the other partner's back is turned. Or to know the one thing the partner doesn't.

And there they were, all the little nuances of expression and body language, visible and accurate.

Not mentioning the fact the scripting did one of the best jobs of getting the essence of things between one medium and another that I've ever seen.

From that time on I figured I was going to do anything I had to do to make it possible for Jane Fancher to continue her project.

She did everything—scripting, blocking, pencils, inking, coloring, *and* the lettering, phone-answering, letter-writing, and business negotiations and promotions— I suspect she'd run the presses if she had to. But Donning has stepped in to give this very remarkable talent a chance to do the things she does best.

I doubt any novelist and graphics artist/scripter have ever worked closer on an adaptation than we have: I have had a marvelous time answering questions and actually providing detail there was no way to put in the novel, simply because there are things the visual medium can do best, and this is the chance to do them.

Through more than a decade now, the **Gate** books have been bringing me letters from readers who have only just come across them—and letters begging me for new ones.

I am glad to see them enter still another medium, at an artistic level I think outstanding in the graphics field.

C.J. Cherryh
Oklahoma City
April, 1987

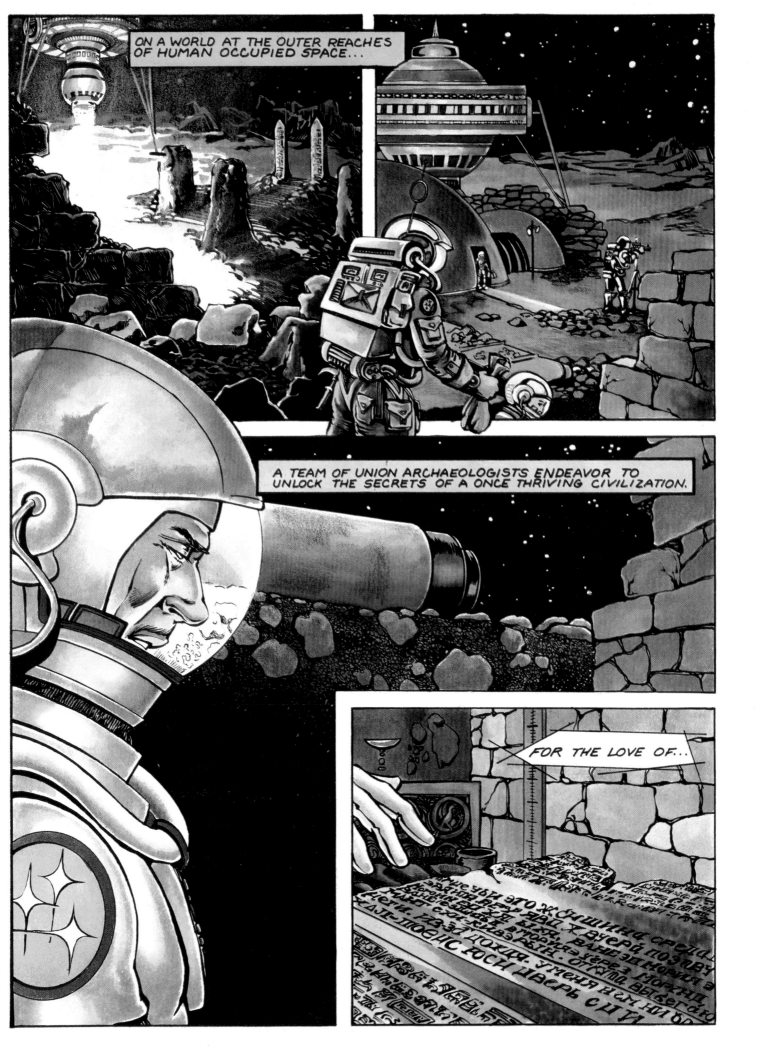

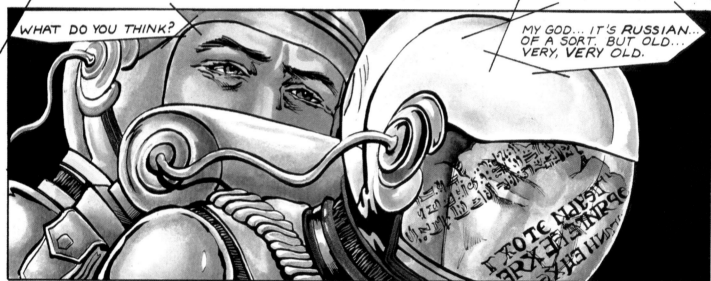

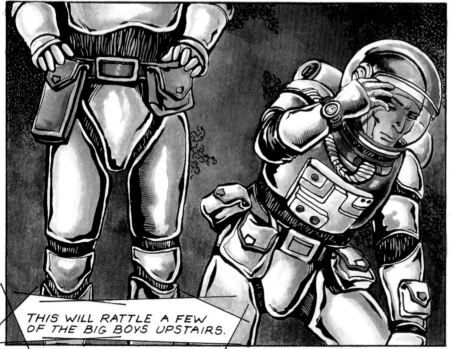

IT SEEMS THE LOCAL INHABITANTS WERE A MIXED LOT. HUMANOID, FROM THE TAPESTRY IN 4-C, BUT NOT ALL THE SAME SPECIES. THE "QHAL" OR "QUJAL" APPEAR TO HAVE BEEN IN TOTAL, IF NOT EXACTLY POPULAR, CONTROL. THOUGH LONG-LIVED AND TECHNOLOGICALLY ADVANCED, THE TRUE KEY TO THEIR DOMINANCE WAS THEIR EXCLUSIVE USE OF THE "GATES."

GATES?

DEVICES WITH SPACE—AND *TIME*—SPANNING CAPABILITIES WHICH ALLOWED THE QHAL TO JUMP INSTANTANEOUSLY...

TO WHEREVER ANOTHER GATE EXISTED.

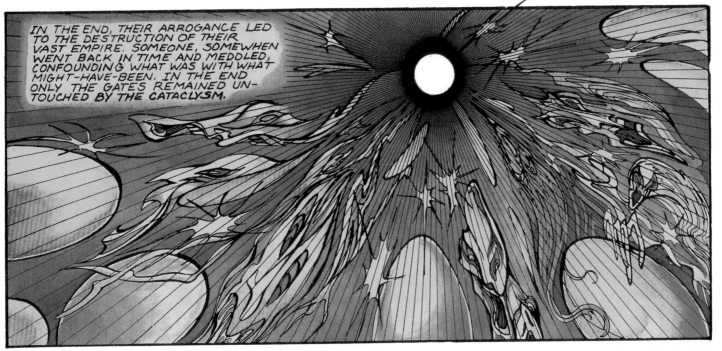

IN THE END, THEIR ARROGANCE LED TO THE DESTRUCTION OF THEIR VAST EMPIRE. SOMEONE, SOMEWHEN WENT BACK IN TIME AND MEDDLED, CONFOUNDING WHAT WAS WITH WHAT MIGHT-HAVE-BEEN. IN THE END ONLY THE GATES REMAINED UN-TOUCHED BY THE CATACLYSM.

GATES. WHAT DO YOU SUPPOSE...

...OH NO...

SAUNDERS!

DON'T TOUCH THA...

STEVEN, YOU'RE ON...

...TWO WAY. HE COULDN'T HEAR YOU.

OPEN BACK UP, IVAN.

ATTENTION! WE ARE HALTING EXCAVATION EFFECTIVE IMMEDIATELY. PACK IT UP AND PREPARE FOR LIFT-OFF.

ON EACH WORLD IN THE GATE NETWORK, THERE WAS ONE MASTER GATE. IF THE GATE LINKAGE STILL EXISTS, EVERY ONE OF THESE WORLD GATES MUST BE DESTROYED.

A SINGLE GATE LEFT ACTIVE COULD REOPEN THE ENTIRE NETWORK AND THE FATE OF THE QHAL COULD BE OURS.

ONCE YOU LEAVE, THIS GATE WILL BE DEACTIVATED AND ALL INFORMATION REGARDING ITS PURPOSE AND USE DESTROYED.

THE MISSION MAY BE OVER WITH THIS FIRST GATE... IT MAY CONTINUE FOR GENERATIONS.

TWO THINGS ARE CERTAIN.

YOU CANNOT AFFORD TO FAIL.

AND THERE CAN BE NO RETURN... NOT FOR YOU...

NOT FOR YOUR CHILDREN.

"THE FUTURE OF MANKIND IS IN YOUR HANDS."

And the winter drawing near,

The Middle Realms

KATH SVEJUR

Ra-Baien· ·Baien-an IrnSvejur

Baien-ei

ALIS KAJE

San-morij   Ra-morij

The human occupied Middle Realms of Andur and Kursh are constantly at war,   the clans at odds since the passing of the High Kings of Koris a hundred years ago... when the King joined strangers from the south in an assault against the Hjemur witch-lord, Thiye, and the loyal clans of the empire mysteriously disappeared into the valley of Irien.

Morija

Luo

Erd

Ra-Le

Ethrih-mri

CEDUR MAJE

Morgaine's Tomb

Pywn

Aenor

N

W   E

S

The Kurshin world is mountains and valleys, horses and herding, its people more closely wedded to both   church and superstition than are their forest dwelling Andurin neighbors... whose roots lie in the elegant courts of the lost High Kings.

Hjemur

IVREL

IRIEN

∴ Ra-Koris

Koris

KE DOMEN

Though separated by the Cedur Maje, a high range of mountains, the ruling clan of Morija, Nhi, has a special hatred for the Chya of Koris, decendants of those High Kings... for Nhi rose to power when Morija's former ruling clan vanished at Irien; and they opposed any attempt from Chya to reunite the Kingdom.

In the reign of Nhi Rijan, this feud led to his capture and imprisonment of a lady of Chya.

She bore him a son: Nhi Vanye... fully acknowledged by Rijan and raised in Ra-Morij alongside his two legitimate Nhi-Myya half-brothers: Kandrys, heir to Rijan, and Erij.

Vanye found his mixed heritage a burden. Neither Chya nor Nhi, he became the source of a thousand suspicions, brutal pranks and cruel innuendo until one day...

DO YOU WISH FOR THAT?

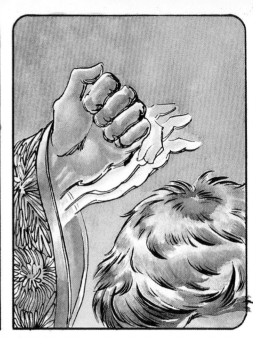

YOU HAVE CHOSEN TO LIVE!

The braid is the mark of Nhi pride and manhood, the right to wear it granted by one's lord and peers. With a few swift strokes of Vanye's own honor blade, Rijan marks his son as a coward and common felon for hanging.

Exile does not demand this further punishment. It is lord Rijan's lasting reminder of unsatisfied Nhi honor.

So, **Lady** Ilel, Ra-Morij is purged of your *Chva* taint at last.

Kandrys! What have I done?

How did we come to this? What was it I did?

When?

You both tolerated me well enough once.

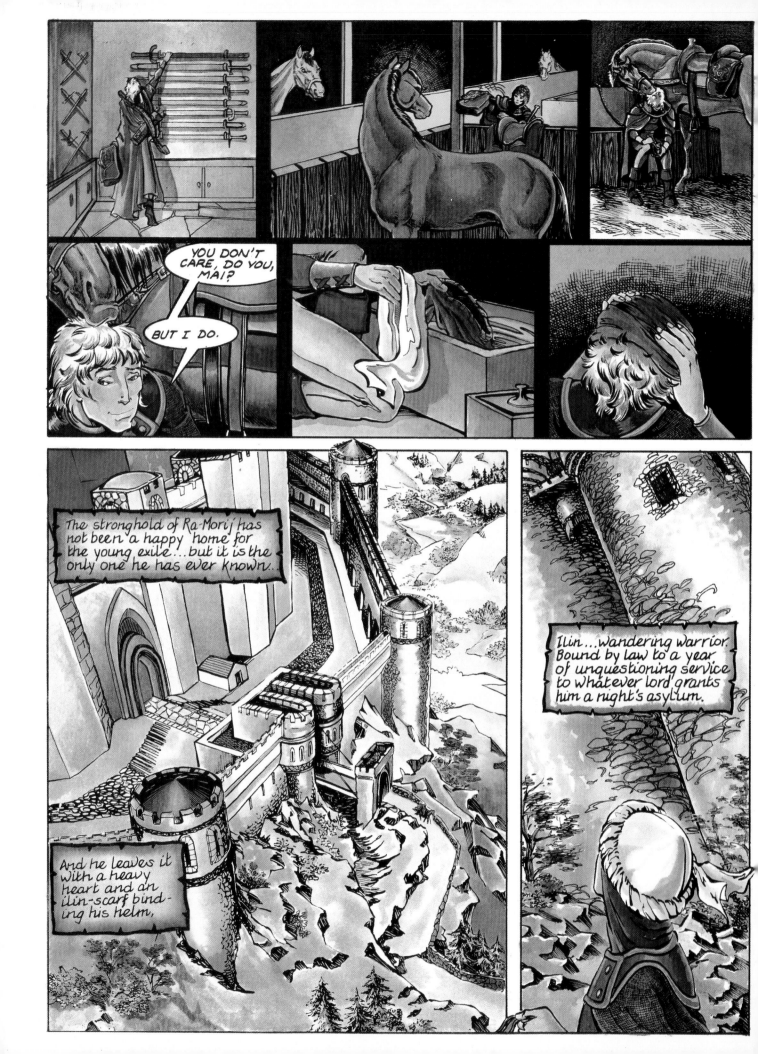

For two years, Vanye struggles simply to survive,

Most ilinin do not. The great wars which had once made an ilin's life profitable exist no longer.

Now there are only petty squabbles between clans and an ilin's life is generally short and miserable. But an ilin who survives his year's service is purged of his disgrace and crimes,

For a time, familiar surroundings provide easy protection and keep Vanye in the mountains of his boyhood... hoping time will cool Myya Gervaine's wrath which keeps Vanye from the possible safety in Aenor. Deeply ashamed, he avoids country-folk and one-time friends alike.

Finally, the cold of winter...

Drives Vanye at last into Gervaine's lands,

Where a Myya arrow...

As well as...

...brings down his beloved Mai...

...Vanye's swift retribution.

But Myya death...

Renews Myya pursuit...

...And from Luo to Ethrith-Mri, they force Vanye South...

...until Aenor, and safety, lie just beyond the next ridges. A fresh blanket of snow chills him to the bone...

...but stops pursuit...   ...he hopes.

Weary and faint with hunger, he sleeps in the saddle as the mare picks her way along the dim trail.

Too late, he realizes the nature of that trail.

Broken pavement underfoot...

Standing stones that line the roadway; road markers placed there by ancient, non-human engineers.

Qujalin...And a path no man would ride with a light heart.

Though none of that old race remain in Andur-Kursh, rumors of their powers and atrocities abound. The very relics of these unholy beings may yet contaminate a god-fearing man's soul.

But the very real threat behind...

...outweighs the less tenable one ahead until his aimless flight brings him to Morgaine's Vale...legend and rumor come to grim reality.

Ten thousand men were led to their doom by the woman who disappeared into this valley a century ago.

Of the five strangers who rallied the High King and his followers against Thiye, only she had survived Irien... only she was not of human blood.

Silver hair and gray eyes...Morgaine Frosthair...only Qujal were thus marked.

Morgaine's tomb...

Even yet it radiates unknown energies which cause skin to crawl...

...and trees to grow twisted... like souls in torment.

More mobile wildlife keeps its distance,

It is the first game Vanye has seen in days...but fatigued muscle and restless horse betray him...

The tomb... something...

A powerful sense of deja vu momentarily stuns him...

As his vision clears...

MORGAINE!?!

Logic denies what he knows to be true.

I KNOW YOU!

OH? HAS THEE COME HUNTING ME?

NO!

COME.

Prudence dictates he set spurs to the mare and run, but Vanye is curiously numb.

WILL YOU DRESS IT...

...OR SHALL I?

QUJALIN WITCHERY!

The buck is quite dead but there is no visible wound.

NHI VANYE--IS THERE A PROBLEM?

NO... NOTHING.

He has no stomach for a thing killed in such a manner...

...but a man would not lose his soul over a bit of venison...

...no matter how the beast was slain.

For the two waiting patiently outside there is scant grain left. The Nhi are breeders of fine horses but Morgaine's Siptah is the last of a breed that perished at Irien and is a treasure in himself to Vanye.

...and her.

BE AT EASE.

THERE IS NO HARM IN WORDS BETWEEN US

WHAT BECAME OF THE MEN I KNEW?

I BEG THEE. TELL ME THE END OF MY TALE.

I WAS NOT ABLE TO KNOW.

Foolish, perhaps, but the night is cold . . . he has already accepted her food...

...And it is a rare and excellent Baien-an wine.

WHAT WAS IT I DID?

I DO NOT THINK THEN...

Hunger and exhaustion have made him dangerously care less. Alone of women, Morgaine, who rode with the lost High King, has the right to claim his services. He has sheltered at her fire as he would have at that of some common farm wife. Such folk have no claim to make against an ilin...

Morgaine does.

LADY, I BEG EXCEPTION.

I WAS GOING TO KINSMEN IN AENOR-PYVVN. I AM EXILED IN EVERY PROVINCE OF MORIJA. I DARE NOT GO BACK THERE. I AM LITTLE HELP TO ANYONE.

AND... THAT IS NOT ALL...

WHY...?

FOR MURDER. F-FOR BROTHER-KILLING.

IT WAS A FIGHT HE FORCED, LADY, BUT I KILLED MY B-BROTHER-- MY HALF-BROTHER. HE WAS NHI-MYYA.

I AM OUT-LAWED AND THERE ARE TWO CLANS WITH BLOOD-DEBT AGAINST ME.

I AM GRATEFUL FOR THE SHELTER, I... THANK YOU. ONLY NAME ME SOME REASON-ABLE SERVICE IN PAYMENT.

YOU CANNOT POSSI-BLY STAY HERE. YOU ARE CURSED IN EVERY HOLD IN ANDUR-KURSH.

YOU HAVE BEEN GENEROUS WITH ME AND I AM GIVING YOU GOOD AD-VICE. LET ME GUIDE YOU... SOMEHOW... TO THE SOUTH OF AENOR WHERE THE LANDS ARE WARM.

THEY ARE SAVAGES THAT LIVE THERE, BUT THEY HAVE NO BLOOD FEUD AGAINST YOU AND YOU WILL BE SAFE.

To yield his soul by breaking the holy oath he made as ilin or to risk it by serving the likes of her.

NO!

For a man who has lost in either case, the only thing left is life. And life is certain to be longer by running...

NOT

YOU!

...then by remaining with Morgaine Frost-hair.

However, even as he bolts, Vanye knows escape to be impossible. The memory of the buck's silent death is still fresh.

IT IS LAWFUL, WHAT I ASK.

A YEAR WITH YOU WILL LIKELY BE MY LAST.

YOUR HAND, ILIN.

MY OWN LIFE IS LIKELY TO BE NO LONGER. I HAVE NO PITY TO SPARE FOR THEE.

Whatever she may, in truth, be, Morgaine knows the human ritual well.

ON YOUR SOUL, ILIN.

ON MY SOUL... LIYO

There is no way back for Vanye now: the ilin oath is holy and transcends all other laws and fealties. His only duty is to obey his liyo's orders.

Legal and moral responsibility for those acts falls on her—his only sin is if he fails to perform to her satisfaction.

But an unscrupulous lord could order many acts personally and morally repugnant to an honorable man—even to sending him against homeland and blood-kin.

Instead of the kind and saintly Aenor in lord with whom Vanye had hoped to serve out his ilin sentence, he finds himself claimed by the devil incarnate: who...

...with his blood and ashes from her hearth...

...marks his palm with the Chya clan-glyph... hers by adoption, his by birth and a clan whose members would as soon see them both dead as not.

CARE FOR THYSELF, THEN, AND GATHER THY GEAR AND MINE. WE ARE LEAVING THIS PLACE.

Changeling: the legends surrounding her sword are almost as dire as those of Morgaine herself.

Changeling: alien and otherly— yet it tempts him.

LET IT BE!

LADY..?

IT IS A GIFT OF ONE OF MY COMPANIONS—A VANITY. IT PLEASED HIM. HE— HAD GREAT SKILL.

BUT IF THEE DISLIKES THINGS QUJALIN, THEN KEEP HANDS FROM IT!

WHERE ARE WE BOUND?

WHERE I WILL GO.

LADY, THIS WAY LIES MORIJ-ERD WHERE MYVA-GERVAINE RULES. HE HAS SWORN TO HAVE MY HEAD ON A PIKE AND...OTHER PARTS OF ME SIMILARLY DISTRIBUTED.

WHAT THEN?

YOU KNOW YOUR WAY WELL ENOUGH. WHY MUST YOU SNARE ME FOR A GUIDE?

WE HEAD EAST BEFORE THEN... TOWARD KORIS.

HOW SHOULD I KNOW OTHERWISE THAT GERVAINE RULES IN ERD? BESIDES, I DID NOT SAY YOU WERE TO BE A GUIDE IN THESE LANDS.

FIREWOOD?

VANYE!

Vanye lays a dampwood fire hoping to coax it into flames, but as he turns for more wood....

HOW...?

To Vanye's relief, the following afternoon brings lower altitudes, sunshine and signs of civilization.

WHAT WAS THIS PLACE?

A FARM. A FAIR AND PLEASANT ONE. I SPENT A NIGHT HERE HARDLY A MONTH AGO.

As Morgaine rides wordlessly on, Vanye continues to ponder the ruins. "A month ago" - her time. But even a hundred years...

Fire? Not a surprising vengeance on people that had sheltered the Witch of Irien.

Simply one of many disasters to occur in her wake.

Most often to the most innocent.

VANYE...!

WHA...!

HA HA HA HA HA HA HA

Next...

Gate of IVREL

FEVER DREAMS

Adapted and illustrated by Jane Fancher
from the novel by C. J. Cherryh

The Starblaze Newsletter keeps you posted on upcoming titles
and other interesting data. (It's free, too!)
Send your name and address to:
Starblaze Newsletter • The Donning Company/Publishers
5659 Virginia Beach Boulevard • Norfolk, Virginia 23502

GRAPHICS

GLOSSARY

Aenor—EYE-nor
Southern Andurin canton (province)

Alis Kaje—ah-LIS KAH-zheh
Northern mountain range border between Baien and Hjemur.

Andur—AN-door
Eastern section of the human-occupied Middle Realms: Lowland with dense forest.

Baien—BYE-en
Northern Kurshin canton.

Cedur Maje—SAY-door MA-zheh
Mountain range border between Andur and Kursh.

Changeling—
Morgaine's sword and as sheathed in mystery as the lady herself. Forged by one of her companions, it has reputedly deadly tendencies.

CHYA—Ch'YAH (all one syllable—just sneeze)
Ruling clan of Koris.

Dai-uyo—DI-OO-yo
High clan "knight." Vanye's forebears came from the same Baltic region, a melting pot of civilizations, which spawned Earth's chivalric, medieval period.

Emory, Ariane—
Twenty-fourth century Union geneticist. Head of Reseune Laboratories.

Erij—EH-ridge
Nhi Erij i Myya: second son to Nhi Rijan.

Gate(s)—
Also called "witchfires." Space-time transport devices installed throughout the Qhal Empire.

Hjemur—HYAY-moor
Northern territory still under Qhalur influence.

Ilel—ee-LEHL
Chya Ilel i Chya: Vanye's mother.

Ilin—EE-lin
Warrior who does penance by service. Capital punishment is not, in general, an acceptable option in Andur-Kursh. An offender of this degree may therefore be sentenced to obligatory service to any lord from whom he accepts food and fire-warmth. That service may be a year of virtual slavery or take the form of a specific task to be performed. The lord acquires any guilt attached to the orders he gives, but the ilin may be badly treated, sent into impossible situations, even killed by his lord without cause or reason. Either way, if he dies in service or lives to complete it, he is absolved of guilt and restored to his former rank. More importantly, since this is a holy oath, he has saved his soul. If he breaks oath, he is damned to hell and only his lord's forgiveness can save him.

Irien—EER-i-ehn
Valley at the base of Ivrel where the Andur-Kursh army led by Morgaine kri Chya and her companions perished. Morgaine was the sole survivor.

Ivrel—iv-REHL
Volcanic peak where the master gate is located.

Kandrys—KAN-dris
Nhi Kandrys i Myya: First son and heir to Rijan.

Koris—KO-ris
Central Anduran canton

Kursh—KURSH
Western section of the human-occupied Middle Realms.

Liyo—LEE-yo
Specialized term for an ilin's liege lord.

Mai—my
Vanye's horse(s). (Our hero lacks a certain flair in these areas.) Actually, his first horse's name was Mai, therefore, lacking any information to the contrary, he calls any other horse he acquires and feels affection for by the same name.

Morgaine—mor-GAYN
Morgaine kri Chya, also known as Morgaine Frosthair: last descendant of the Union task force sent to destroy the Gates. Sole survivor of the disaster at Irien, she has, by Vanye's time, assumed demonic proportions in Kurshin legend. The kri Chya indicates adoption by the clan Chya.

Morija—mor-IH-zhah
Central Kurshin canton.

Myya—m'YAH
Minor clan of Morija. Known for its suspicious and politically ambitious court.

Myya Gervaine—m'YAH gehr-VAYN
Head of Myya clan and uncle to Kandrys and Erij.

Nhi—n'HEE
Ruling clan of Morija.

Pyvvn—PIH-v'n
Central stronghold of Aenor.

Qhal—Khal (KH is pronounced as CH in Loch Ness or ach-tung). Ancient interstellar travellers responsible for current gate network.

Qujal—kih-YAHL
Kurshin term for Qhal.

Qujalin—kih-YAHL-in
Adjectival form of Qujal.

Ra-Morij—RAH-MO-rizh
Central stronghold of Morija.

Reseune—reh-ZUOON
Center of Union's biological and psychological research in genetic engineering and cloning.

Rijan—ree-ZHAHN
Nhi Rijan ii Nhi: Father to Vanye, Kandrys and Erij, ruler of Nhi clan (and, therefore, all of Morija).

Ris Gir—REES JEER
Leader of "posse" sent after Morgaine kri Chya following the disaster at Irien.

San Romen—SAN RO-mehn
Chief armorer of Ra-Morij.

Siptah—SIP-tah
Morgaine's Baien-bred war-trained stallion.

Thiye—THEE-yeh
Lord of Hjemur.

Union—
One of the three primary human political powers in the twenty-fourth century.

Uyo—OO-yo
Status somewhat equivalent to medieval knighthood.

Vanye—VAHN-yeh
Nhi Vanye i Chya: illegitimate son of Rijan and Ilel.

AFTERWORD

"Hello" from Jane Fancher and Venus

There is a popular saying going around these days: Life's a (fill in appropriate negative phraseology)...then you die. Well, either the statement is totally kerwhacky, or I've died and gone to heaven.

How else is it that after years of doing the nine-to-five (and all too often the eight-to-twenty-two) routine, fighting rush hour traffic and cultivating a fine crop of ulcers, I find myself playing fifteen hours a day in my own backyard, with some of the most delightful and creative people the world has to offer as my playmates and getting paid for it in the bargain? Fate has indeed been kind in allowing me to produce the adaptation of **Gate of Ivrel** for you—but so have a number of special individuals whose help I truly wish to acknowledge here:

1. To my long-suffering family and friends who have endured the obsessive behavior inherent to someone shoving fifteen years of learning into four: I love you and am sorry, but it's not over yet!

2. To the distributors and storeowners who carried the original black and white version of **Gate** and those lovely folks who bought it: thank you for your encouragement and support and thank goodness I'm not going that route any longer!

3. To all the various publishers: WaRP for introducing me to this crazy business, DAW for their patience and cooperation, and all the folks at Donning/Starblaze for their patient understanding and for giving me this opportunity to realize the dream. I hope you agree it was worth the effort.

Specifically:

1. To Lynn Kingsley and Gail Butler who loaned me their specialized talents and saved me a great deal of research time: Ladies, you're wonderful! (...and now, for the *next* book...!)

2. To my editor, Kay Reynolds, whose every comment was invaluable, who knew when to give in and when not and whose clear-eyed vision of the potential of the graphic novel is so very exciting to aim for: my friend, you're one in a million.

3. To Carolyn J. Cherryh who has graciously loaned me her charming characters and their story and who has from the beginning given me her friendship and support: Ms. Cherryh, ma'am, not only could I NOT do this without you... I wouldn't want to.

Finally:

To all the university art department personnel who looked down very long noses at a physics major who wanted to take a few art classes: Thanks for not letting me in.

Now the kids and I must get back to work...long hours are never half as long as we see by the clock while we have a story we love to work on with people we love to work with. All I can think to say is, Life may not be a bed of roses but it sure can be a lot of fun if we give it a chance.

Jane Fancher
Renton, Washington
May, 1987